Antonie Schneider

Come Back, Pigeon!

Illustrated by Uli Waas

Translated by J. Alison James

North-South Books

NEW YORK · LONDON

Copyright © 1999 by Nord-Süd Verlag AG, Gossau Zürich, Switzerland.
First published in Switzerland under the title *Eine Taube für Bollibar*
English translation copyright © 1999 by North-South Books Inc.

First published in the United States, Great Britain, Canada,
Australia, and New Zealand in 1999 by North-South Books,
an imprint of Nord-Süd Verlag AG, Gossau Zürich, Switzerland.
First paperback edition published in 2001.

Distributed in the United States by North-South Books Inc., New York.

Library of Congress Cataloging-in-Publication Data
Schneider, Antonie.
[Taube für Bollibar. English]
Come back, pigeon! / by Antonie Schneider; illustrated by Uli Waas;
translated by J. Alison James.
p.   cm.
Summary: When the pigeon Barnaby buys shortly after his family
moves to the country flies away, he and his sister Flora begin to
help an elderly neighbor care for his flock of pigeons.
[1. Pigeons—Fiction.] I. Waas, Uli, ill.
II. James, J. Alison. III. Title.
PZ7.S3617Co 1999
[E]—dc21   99-12677

A CIP catalogue record for this book is available
from The British Library.

ISBN 0-7358-1140-7 (TRADE BINDING)
1 3 5 7 9 TB 10 8 6 4 2
ISBN 0-7358-1141-5 (LIBRARY BINDING)
1 3 5 7 9 LB 10 8 6 4 2
ISBN 0-7358-1416-3 (PAPERBACK)
1 3 5 7 9 PB 10 8 6 4 2
Printed in Belgium

For more information about our books,
and the authors and artists who create them,
visit our web site: www.northsouth.com

Flora and Barnaby sat on the old garden wall enjoying the warm September sun.

They had moved from the city to their new house in the country a few weeks ago. How different life in the country was!

"Look there—swallows," said Flora.

"And here come some pigeons!" cried Barnaby. "They're landing right next door!"

The pigeons all flocked around old
Gabriel. He stood under his apple tree
and let the pigeons land on him.

Flora was astonished. "They're so tame!"

Barnaby stared. "Look, they're even
eating out of his hand."

Suddenly Barnaby jumped off the wall and disappeared into the house.

In a minute he came out again with his piggy bank tucked under his arm.

"Hey, where are you going?" Flora called.

Barnaby didn't answer. He ran up the
path to town.

"Barnaby! Wait for me!" cried Flora.

But her brother had already disappeared.

Flora climbed back up on the wall and
sat wondering where he'd gone.

When Barnaby returned, he held a
pigeon carefully in both hands.

"This is Jewel," he said. "My pet pigeon.
I bought her in the village."

"What will Mother say?" said Flora.

They heard footsteps on the path.
"Come on! We'd better hide her,"
whispered Barnaby.

They ran into the shed and shut
the door.

"I have to get a few things," said
Barnaby. "To make Jewel a nesting box."
He set the pigeon carefully on the ground
and ran out. "Take care of her," he cried.

Jewel fluttered excitedly among the garden tools.

"Jewel," whispered Flora. "Jewel, this is your new home. We'll take good care of you."

Jewel fluttered and cooed and hopped around. Finally she landed in a half-opened umbrella and was still.

Then Barnaby came back with a shoe box filled with straw. He set it on the table.

Barnaby put some grain in the nest.
He carefully put the pigeon in.

"Come on," Flora said. "We have to
leave her alone now so she settles down."
And she pulled Barnaby out of the shed.

They went back outside and played ball.
Now and again they peeked though the
shed window.

Every time they looked, Jewel was
sitting in her box. She never moved.

Finally Barnaby said, "I hope she's okay."

Flora was worried too. "Let's ask Gabriel."

The old man was sitting at his window.

"Good idea," said Barnaby. "He'll know
for sure if she's all right."

They climbed over the wall into
Gabriel's garden. The door to his house
stood open. Barnaby knocked.

Gabriel called, "Come in! I'm glad you stopped by. How are you settling into your new home?"

"Fine," answered Barnaby and Flora at the same time.

Gabriel laughed. "Would you like a mint?" he asked. He passed them a jar with a ship on the lid.

Barnaby said: "We came here
because of Jewel."

Gabriel coughed. "Because of Jewel?"
he asked. He went to the window and
pointed. "Is that lady coming out of your
shed there Jewel?"

"Oh, no! Flora, look!" Barnaby cried.
Their mother left the shed door open
and Jewel flew out right behind her.

Jewel soared and swooped in circles over the apple tree, flying higher and higher.

"Jewel!" cried Barnaby and Flora, horrified. "Jewel!"

At last the pigeon was only a tiny gray point that disappeared between the clouds.

Gabriel stood by the two children in the garden.

"So that was Jewel. How she can fly!" he said, with awe in his voice. "What a wonderful thing it would be to fly like that."

The funny thing was, Gabriel never said: You shouldn't have bought a pigeon. What a waste of money! A pigeon is not a stuffed toy! He didn't say anything like that at all. He just stood there with the two children, staring into the sky where Jewel had disappeared.

Then a flock of swallows landed chattering and chirping in the apple tree.

Gabriel shook his head and smiled. "Come, children, I have something to show you."

Barnaby and Flora followed Gabriel up some steep stairs. "Here is where I keep my pigeons. It's called a dovecote," he said.

The children were sad because Jewel had flown away. But they were also curious about Gabriel's pigeons.

When they were at the top, Gabriel said, "Don't worry about Jewel. Pigeons can fly quite far, even across oceans. But they always come back to their home."

"But Jewel was home with us for only a few hours," Flora said.

"Well, that might be a problem," said Gabriel. "But you can always share my pigeons. I could use the help."

So Gabriel showed the children what to
do. And from then on, Flora and Barnaby
had an after-school job. They cleaned the
nests. They poured fresh water into bowls.
They filled boxes with grain. And they
sat for hours at the window listening to
Gabriel tell stories about his pigeons. As
the winter passed, they took on more and
more of the work.

One day Barnaby said, "Look! The swallows are building a nest!"

It was springtime and the swallows had come back.

"How time has flown," said Gabriel.

Up in the dovecote, the pigeons fluttered and cooed.

"I think they're glad it's spring," said Barnaby.

"You're right," agreed Flora. "They do look very happy."

Just then a pigeon landed right on Barnaby's hand.

"Look!" he said softly.

"Pigeons are very wise," said Gabriel. "You took good care of them all winter and have earned their trust."

Barnaby smiled happily.

One morning in early summer, Gabriel wasn't sitting at the window. He was still asleep in bed. Flora and Barnaby sat down beside him.

"Maybe he's dreaming of flying," whispered Barnaby.

Then Gabriel woke up. "Oh hello," he said. "I'm not feeling very well today."

"Don't worry," said Flora. "We can take care of the pigeons."

"I know you can," he said, smiling. "How good that you are here."

Suddenly they heard something pecking at the window.

Flora and Barnaby stared in amazement.

"She's a bit bigger," said Barnaby, "but she looks exactly like Jewel!"

"Gabriel said she'd come back," said Flora, "but I never thought she would. Do you think it's really Jewel?"

"I'm sure of it!" said Barnaby. "That's the wonderful thing about pigeons. They always come back!"

About the Author

Antonie Schneider was born in Mindelheim, in southern Germany. A former schoolteacher, she is the author of three picture books, *Luke the Lionhearted*; *You Shall Be King!*; and *Good-Bye, Vivi!*; and one other easy-to-read book, *The Birthday Bear*, all published by North-South.

About the Illustrator

Uli Waas was born in Donauworth, Bavaria. She studied painting and graphics at the Academy of Graphic Arts in Munich. Since then she has illustrated many books for children, including five other easy-to-read books for North-South: *Where's Molly?*, *Spiny*, *A Mouse in the House!*, *The Ghost in the Classroom*, and *The Birthday Bear*.

NORTH-SOUTH PAPERBACK EASY-TO-READ BOOKS